Josh's Sh

Story by Annette Smith

Illustrations by Samantha Asri

Josh said to Lily,

"Come into my shop.

It is a good shop."

milk
butter
cheese
eggs
rice

"I'm looking for some bread," said Lily.

"No bread today," said Josh.

5

"Where are the eggs, Josh?"
said Lily.
"I cannot see the eggs."

"No eggs today," said Josh.

"My baby likes bananas,"
said Lily.
"Where are the bananas?"

"No bananas today," said Josh.

"This is **not** a good shop," said Lily.

"No bread … no eggs … and no bananas!"

11

"My baby is hungry," said Lily.

"Look!" said Josh.

"Here are some ice cream bars."

milk

butter

cheese

eggs

rice

"Here is an ice cream bar
 for your baby," said Josh.

"My baby is too little
 to eat an ice cream bar," said Lily.
"I will eat it."

"I will eat this ice cream bar!"
said Josh.